EGMONT

We bring stories to life

First published in Great Britain in 2016 by Egmont UK Limited
The Yellow Building, 1 Nicholas Road, London W11 4AN

DreamWorks Trolls © 2016 DreamWorks Animation LLC. All Rights Reserved.

Written by Paddy Kempshall
Designed by Katie Scruton & Miffy Llwyd-Williams

ISBN 978 1 4052 8350 2
63788/1
Printed in Italy

Parental guidance is advised for all craft and colouring activities. Always ask an adult to help when using glue,
paint and scissors. Wear protective clothing and cover surfaces to avoid staining.

Stay safe online. Egmont is not responsible for content hosted by third parties.

Contents

DreamWorks

Trolls

Annual 2017

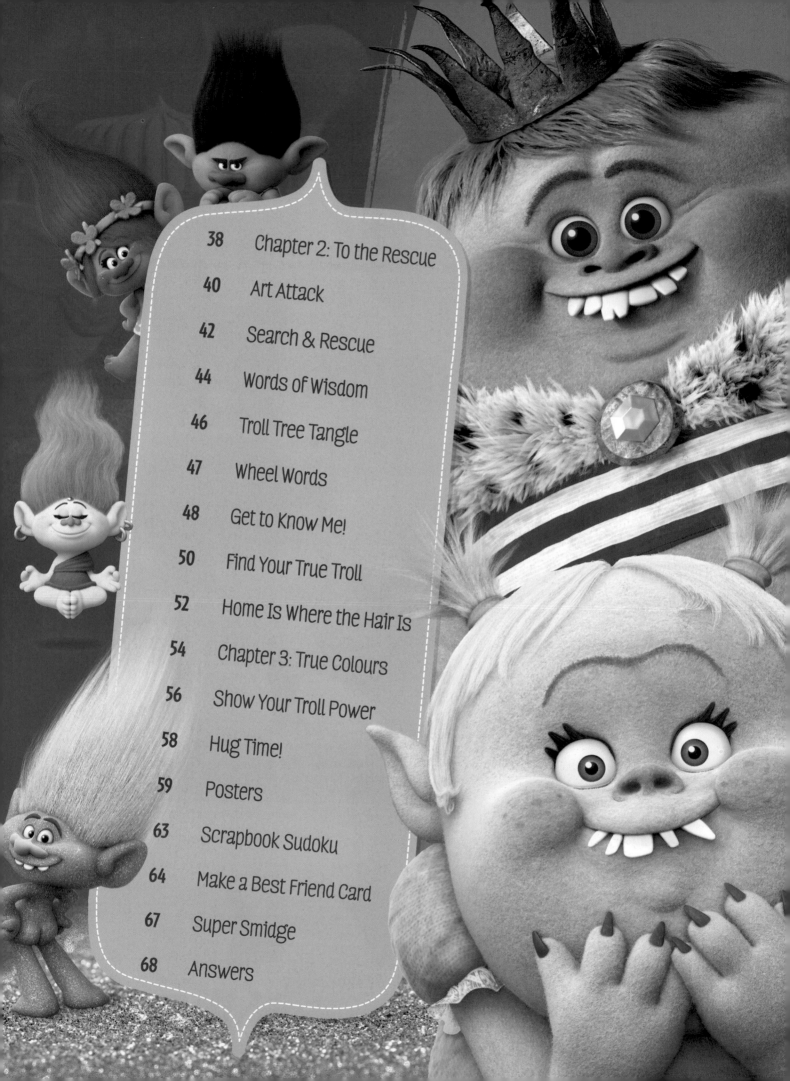

Get to Know
POPPY

Beautiful pink hair

You'll **KNOW** her by:

Hair-mazing headband

Huge smile. ALL THE TIME

If most Trolls are optimistic, **Poppy** is positively Poptimistic!

Princess Poppy is about to be crowned Queen and will do anything to make sure she makes Troll Town the danciest, huggiest, crazy-happiest place EVER!

Poppy likes:

- Her friends
- Ringing her special cowbell
- Singing
- Hugging
- Dancing
- Did we mention the singing thing?

Her fab friends

8

Poppy's BIG BOOK of Hugs

Today, every time Poppy hugged a Troll, she put their picture in her scrapbook!

How many hugs did Poppy give out?

Check your answers on page 68.

Which Troll has Poppy hugged the MOST?

Biggie

a

Fuzzbert

b

Cooper

c

Get to Know
BRANCH

Branch is probably the most un-Troll-like Troll in Troll Town.

Very practical and always ready for anything, he thinks the other Trolls' crazy-happy lifestyle leaves them horribly unprepared for any future Bergen attacks.

You'll **KNOW** him by:

Un-fun dark hair

Grumpy grimace

Camouflage colours

Very untwinkly toes. *No dancing here*

Branch likes:

* Being prepared
* Being careful
* Keeping an eye out for danger

#HUG-FREE ZONE

Branch DOES NOT like:

* Hugging
* Dancing
* Singing
* Hugging again

Branch's typical day

1. Wake up

2. Check it's actually day because he lives in an underground bunker

3. Check how much food is in the panic room

4. Go out and try to warn the other Trolls about the Bergens

5. Dodge Poppy's hugs

6. Watch other Trolls sing and dance

7. Sigh

8. Dodge Poppy's hugs again

9. Sigh some more

10. Head back to bed

Which path should Branch take to hide from the hugs?

a   b   c

Check your answer on page 68.

Get to Know
THE TROLLS

This stylish, clever, glamorous and glittery bunch are Poppy's closest friends and have all found their True Colours!

CREEK

Creek is what's known as a Troll's Troll – he's positive, supportive and super-cool.

Guys want to be him, and all the girls want to be around him. He always seems to know what to say to cheer up others and when he sings, everyone listens!

Glittery freckles

Stylish green hat

COOPER

If you're looking for a Troll to bust out some amazing dance moves, then **Cooper** is the Troll for you.

One of the friendliest Trolls around, he can even show Poppy a thing or two about how to always be full of energy! His full coat of hair is also pretty special, even for a Troll!

Mr Dinkles!

BIGGIE

Biggie really is the gentle giant of the group. Sensitive and caring, he's never scared of showing how he feels or having a good cry.

Biggie always carries around his pet caterpillar, **Mr Dinkles**, and just loves to dress him up. Almost as much as he loves eating cupcakes!

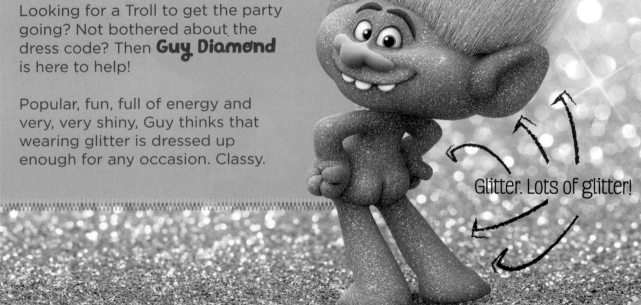

GUY DIAMOND

Looking for a Troll to get the party going? Not bothered about the dress code? Then **Guy Diamond** is here to help!

Popular, fun, full of energy and very, very shiny, Guy thinks that wearing glitter is dressed up enough for any occasion. Classy.

Glitter. Lots of glitter!

Tickle tip

FUZZBERT

Fuzzbert is a bit of a mystery. The other Trolls aren't quite sure what's going on under all that hair, but they do know it seems kind of hard for him to hear in there!

If there are two things which Fuzzbert loves to do, it's dancing and tickling. Not necessarily in that order.

SATIN & CHENILLE

The most fashionable Trolls in town, **Satin & Chenille**, know everything there is to know about looking good. They helped Poppy with her outfits for her coronation.

Even though they're joined by their hair, these Trolls are all about doing their own thing, and will never been seen wearing the same outfits!

Satin is pink

Chenille is blue

DJ SUKI

When singing and dancing are a big part of your day, it helps to have a music master like **DJ Suki** around.

Never without her headphones, she uses her collection of musical crickets, beetles and other little bugs to bash out amazing beats for any occasion.

Hip headphones

Stage bug

Super-strong hair

SMIDGE

She may be small but with her deep, booming voice, **Smidge** is a real powerhouse. She loves to keep fit and really looks after herself, particularly by using her own hair as a skipping rope!

Smidge's hobbies include weightlifting and crochet.

Welcome to
TROLL TOWN

POPULATION: CRAZY-HAPPY

Imagine the most colourful, musical, huggable, friendly place EVER – that's Troll Town.

After King Peppy led them in an escape from the Bergens, the Trolls settled in the forest and built Troll Town. Now they spend their days singing, dancing, hugging and just letting their happy show!

The happiest Troll of all is Soon-to-be-Queen Poppy, who thinks there's no such thing as too many hugs!

With Trolls, love is always in the hair and it's Hug Time every hour, on the hour. Now, if only the Bergens felt the same and stopped trying to eat them ...

Did you know?

In Troll Town cupcakes aren't just a snack, they're a way of life!

The Show Must Go On!

Can you find all the names in the grid and help Poppy round up the Trolls for a big musical number?

 **Biggie**
 **Satin**
 **Chenille**
 **Guy Diamond**
 **Cooper**

 **DJ Suki**
 **Smidge**
 **Harper**
 **Branch**
 **Karma**

The names could be written in any direction!

e	t	s	a	t	b	h	t	r	i	r	h	n	n	e
i	l	n	b	a	t	c	s	f	l	h	e	t	e	o
h	h	l	r	e	e	n	u	r	i	e	g	u	i	q
a	u	e	i	e	t	a	r	n	o	s	o	r	g	f
r	o	s	o	n	a	r	s	a	e	d	a	i	g	e
p	e	r	t	m	e	b	r	e	p	o	o	c	i	e
e	h	s	r	e	t	h	o	t	s	e	h	g	b	e
r	n	a	o	n	r	i	c	e	n	t	y	e	i	s
h	k	u	l	e	e	y	r	r	l	l	o	k	a	t
e	o	s	w	s	e	d	u	r	i	b	u	t	n	m
d	n	o	m	a	i	d	y	u	g	s	i	t	e	c
s	t	e	l	i	o	o	r	f	j	n	e	r	a	b
e	t	e	l	r	d	r	d	d	y	e	n	e	t	t
h	h	h	n	v	i	g	r	t	o	d	h	c	z	m
h	t	o	a	s	a	t	e	n	a	n	r	e	n	e

Check your answers on page 68.

Double Trouble

Harper loves getting arty and has made a change to one of these pictures of Poppy and Cooper. Can you spot the one she changed?

a

b

c

d

e

Check your answer on page 68.

Who Needs a Hug?

Poppy is cutting up some old photos to make a scrapbook of her best hugs ever!

Look at the pieces and put a cross next to the ones which don't appear in the picture.

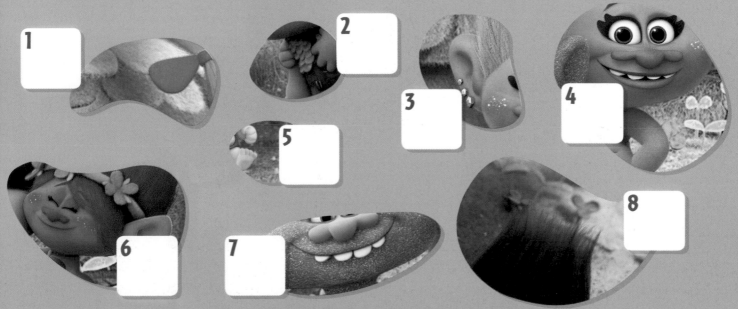

1

2

3

4

5

6

7

8

Check your answer on page 68.

Welcome to BERGEN TOWN

Bergen Town couldn't be more different than the home of the Trolls. Set on the other side of the forest to Troll Town, it's a busy place, full of creatures who are unhappy 364 days of the year.

Bergens are large, lumbering creatures who think they're actually quite fancy.

The one day a year the Bergens are happy is on Trollstice. Then they do the one thing which they just love to do – eat Trolls!

That was until all the Trolls escaped ...

Did you know?

Chef, the King's cook, makes an amazing Troll meatloaf for Trollstice!

Nightmare Neighbour

Trolls need to know what a real Bergen looks like so they can avoid it!

Can you spot the 12 differences between these pictures of Chef and King Gristle?

meet the
BERGENS

Big, greedy and miserable, the Bergens are always looking for a way to find the Trolls and get their happy back.

KING GRISTLE

After an unhappy Trollstice as a child, **King Gristle** became determined to try and bring happiness back to his people.

He thinks that Trolls are the secret to this, but maybe not in the way that he expects ...

Royal crown and fluffy cape

Did you know?

King Gristle is a great roller skater and won't sit down to eat without a fresh, new bib!

BRIDGET

Bridget is the helper and washer-up in the Royal Kitchens. Unlike other Bergens, she is kind-hearted and very nice to others.

She is secretly romantic and wants nothing more than to find happiness in a different way to all the other Bergens.

There's a hairy snack hiding on these pages. Can you spot it?

Lovely smile. For a Bergen ...

Pack for captured Trolls

CHEF

If there's one Bergen who loves Trolls more than anyone, it's **Chef**. She loves them covered in butter, spread on toast, pretty much any way she can eat the tasty little treats!

But after all the Trolls escaped on her watch, Chef finds herself wandering the forest searching for their hidden home.

That's HAIR-MAZING!

Bring out your inner Troll and design some super new hairstyles for Poppy's coronation.

Guy Diamond says: PASS THE GLITTER!

Try drawing a whole new shape for Poppy's hair!

Remember: With Trolls, when it comes to hairstyles it's go big or go home!

25

Chapter 1:
Troll Town

Once upon a time, in a happy forest, lived the happiest creatures the world has ever known ... the Trolls. They loved nothing more than to sing, dance and hug, until, one day, the miserable Bergens found them.

The Bergens were always grumpy and sad. But that was before they found the one thing that made them happy ... eating Trolls!

So the Bergens put a cage around the Troll Tree and, once a year on Trollstice, there was a huge Troll feast.

But this one Trollstice, when young Prince Gristle was to have his first taste of Troll, the Trolls escaped, leaving the Bergens grumpier than ever before!

Fleeing to the forest, King Peppy and the Trolls founded Troll Town and lived there for many years, dancing, singing and hugging their happy lives away.

Now, many years later, King Peppy's daughter, Poppy, is getting ready to become Queen.

"It's going to be the biggest, loudest, craziest party ever!" cry Poppy's friends.

"You're just going to lead the Bergens straight to us!" warns Branch.

But none of the other Trolls want to listen. Branch is always warning them that the Bergens are coming, but they never do.

"I just want all Trolls to be happy!" says Poppy.

Branch, however, still thinks it's a bad idea and refuses to come to the party.

That night, the Trolls celebrate Queen Poppy's coronation. There's lots of loud music, singing, dancing, glitter and a huge fireworks display. Everyone has a great time ... until a Bergen called Chef, who has been searching for the Trolls in the forest, sees the party and comes crashing out of the trees.

Smashing through Troll Town, Chef scoops up Poppy's friends before they can hide.

"You Trolls have made me so happy," she smiles, stomping off into the forest. "And I haven't even eaten you yet!"

After the dust settles, Poppy rushes off to the only Troll she thinks can help rescue her friends – Branch.

"But they're *your* friends," says Branch. "I'm staying right here in my bunker where it's safe."

Branch soon changes his mind though when Poppy invites all the other Trolls to come and stay in his bunker too!

Turn to page 38 to continue the adventure.

IT'S SHOW TIME!

Play the game, gather the Trolls and see if you can help organise Poppy's coronation before time runs out!

1 START

2

3

Cupcake time! Use the energy to zoom on 2 spaces.

HOW TO PLAY

1. Roll the dice and move around the board, following the instructions as you go.

2. Put a cross in a box below for every turn you take.

3. If you fill in all the boxes before you reach the finish, then time's up and it's game over!

18

Dig those tunes and dash on 2 spaces.

19 SO SHINY! BLINDED BY GUY'S BUTT! Cross off another box.

17

16

15 Who needs a HUG? Feel hair-mazing and move on 2 spaces.

14 BERGEN ALERT!

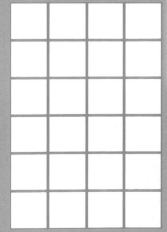

28

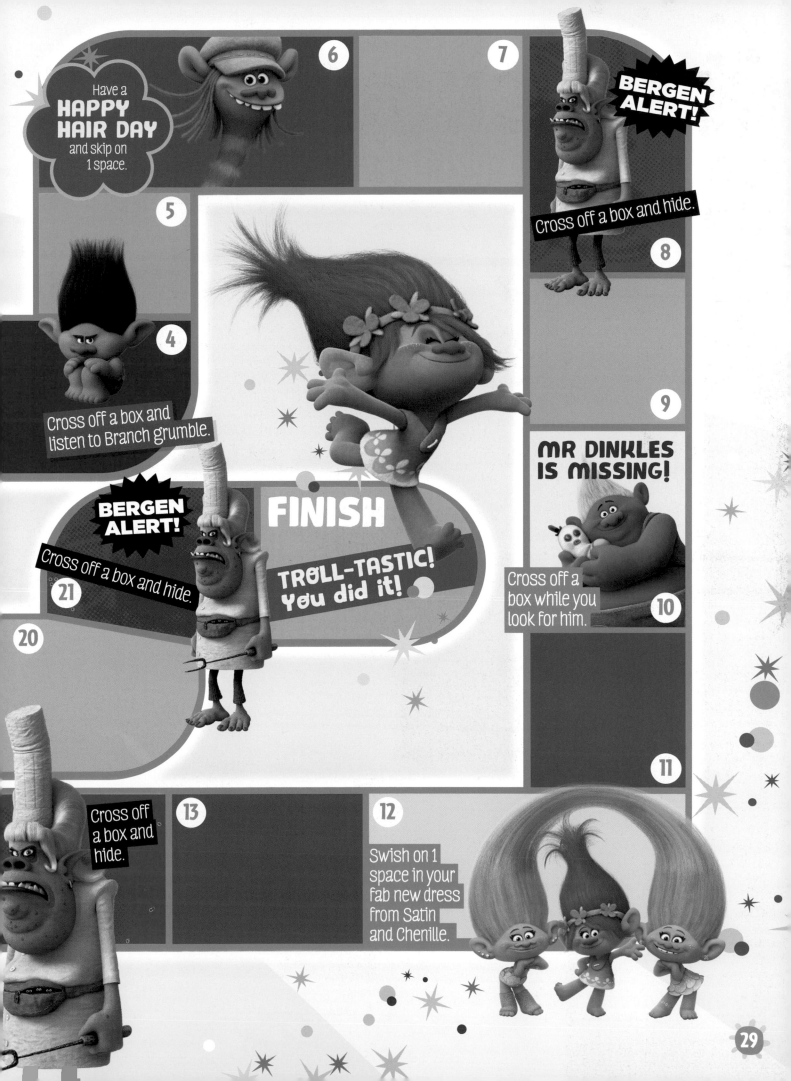

6

Have a
HAPPY HAIR DAY
and skip on 1 space.

7

BERGEN ALERT!

Cross off a box and hide.

8

5

9

4

Cross off a box and listen to Branch grumble.

MR DINKLES IS MISSING!

Cross off a box while you look for him.

10

BERGEN ALERT!

Cross off a box and hide.

21

FINISH

TROLL-TASTIC! You did it!

20

11

Cross off a box and hide.

13

12

Swish on 1 space in your fab new dress from Satin and Chenille.

Troll Teasers

Give your brain a big hug and see if you can figure out these picture puzzles.

Figure out the pattern and then write the number of the cupcake you think comes next.

Can you spot which TWO PICTURES in each row are a pair?

1

2

3

4

Need a Cupcake?

Biggie loves a good cupcake. Get your creative hair on and design the superest, tastiest, Trolliest cupcake for him here.

Why not ...
Cut up some old magazines or wallpaper and make a collage cupcake?

Hide and Seek

Branch is always trying to find better ways to avoid the Bergens. Can you help him with his camouflage skills?

Where is Branch hiding? Starting in section 1A, follow the directions at the top of page 35, moving from square to square to see if you can find Branch.

	1	2	3	4	5	6	7	8
A	START							
B								
C								
D								
E								
F								
G								
H								
I								
J								

⬆ Up
⬇ Down
⬅ Left
➡ Right

Branch is hiding in section:

Check your answer on page 68.

Directions:

➡ 2, ⬇ 7, ➡ 4, ⬆ 1, ➡ 7, ⬇ 3, ➡ 4, ⬆ 4, ➡ 2,

⬆ 2, ⬅ 3, ⬆ 3, ⬅ 3, ⬇ 2, ➡ 1, ⬇ 2, ⬅ 8, ⬆ 2.

| 9 | 10 | 11 | 12 | 13 | 14 | 15 | 16 | 17 | 18 | 19 | 20 |

TASTY TROLLS

Chef is on the lookout for some ingredients for her amazing Trollstice meatloaf. Follow the tangled lines and help her find some tasty Trolls for her recipe.

a

b

c

d

Check your answer on page 69.

Chapter 2:
To the Rescue

Trollstice is back! When King Gristle sees that Chef has returned with some Trolls, he's so happy that he declares Trollstice will return the very next day.

"That's right," he cries. "Happiness is back on the menu!"

Meanwhile, Poppy and Branch creep through the forest, towards Bergen Town.

With a little help from a strange talking cloud, they find their way through the old escape tunnels from the Troll Tree and into the Royal Palace.

"They're alive!" Poppy cries with glee, as she spots her friends from her hiding place.

"Go on, eat, King Gristle," grins Chef and hands him Creek the Troll. And before Poppy and Branch can do anything, King Gristle pops Creek into his mouth!

Branch thinks Creek has been eaten, but Poppy refuses to give up on her friend. Spotting Bridget the kitchen helper carrying away the other Trolls, Poppy follows close behind with Branch.

They soon discover that Bridget isn't like the other Bergens – and she's in love with King Gristle!

"What does it matter?" sniffs Bridget. "It's not like he even knows I'm alive!"

Suddenly Poppy has a great idea. If the Trolls give Bridget an amazing makeover, she can get close to the King and find out what happened to Creek.

"What do you say, Bridget," smiles Poppy. "You get us Creek, and we get you a date with the King!"

So, disguising themselves as a colourful wig, the Trolls climb onto Bridget's head and help turn her into the amazing Lady Glittersparkles.

"Wow," gasps King Gristle when he spots her. "Would you care to join me for an evening at Captain Starfunkle's Mini-Golf, Roller Rink and Arcade?"

On the date, things seem to be going to plan when King Gristle shows Bridget his pendant – which has Creek trapped inside! Even better for Bridget, he then invites Lady Glittersparkles to join him at the Trollstice feast!

Just then, Chef arrives. Bridget starts to worry that she will be recognised, so she quickly runs off, leaving only a roller skate behind her.

"I miss Lady Glittersparkles already," sighs King Gristle.

Turn to page 54 to finish the story.

ART Attack

Test your drawing skills by using the grid to help you finish these pictures of Poppy's pals.

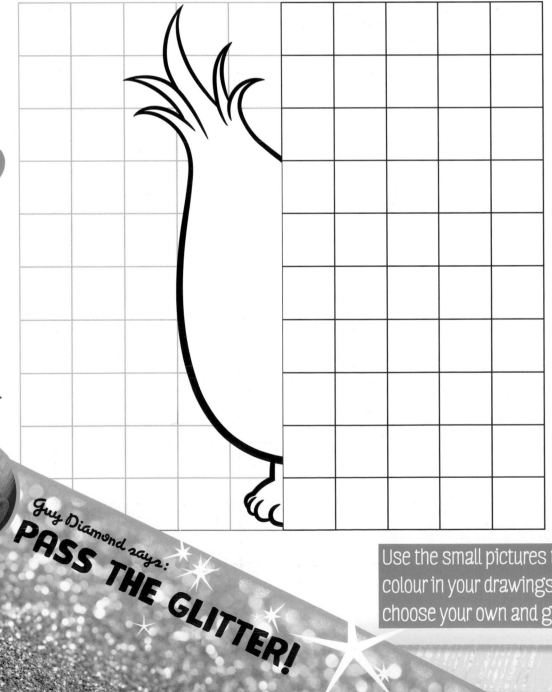

Guy Diamond says:
PASS THE GLITTER!

Use the small pictures to help colour in your drawings, or choose your own and get creative!

SEARCH & RESCUE

Quick! How fast can you find your way through the maze and help Poppy and Branch rescue their Troll friends?

Start

Watch out for King Gristle and Chef!

42

Finish

Check your answer on page 69.

WORDS OF WISDOM

Cybil loves to share her advice with anyone who'll listen!
Can you crack the code and work out one of her favourite sayings?

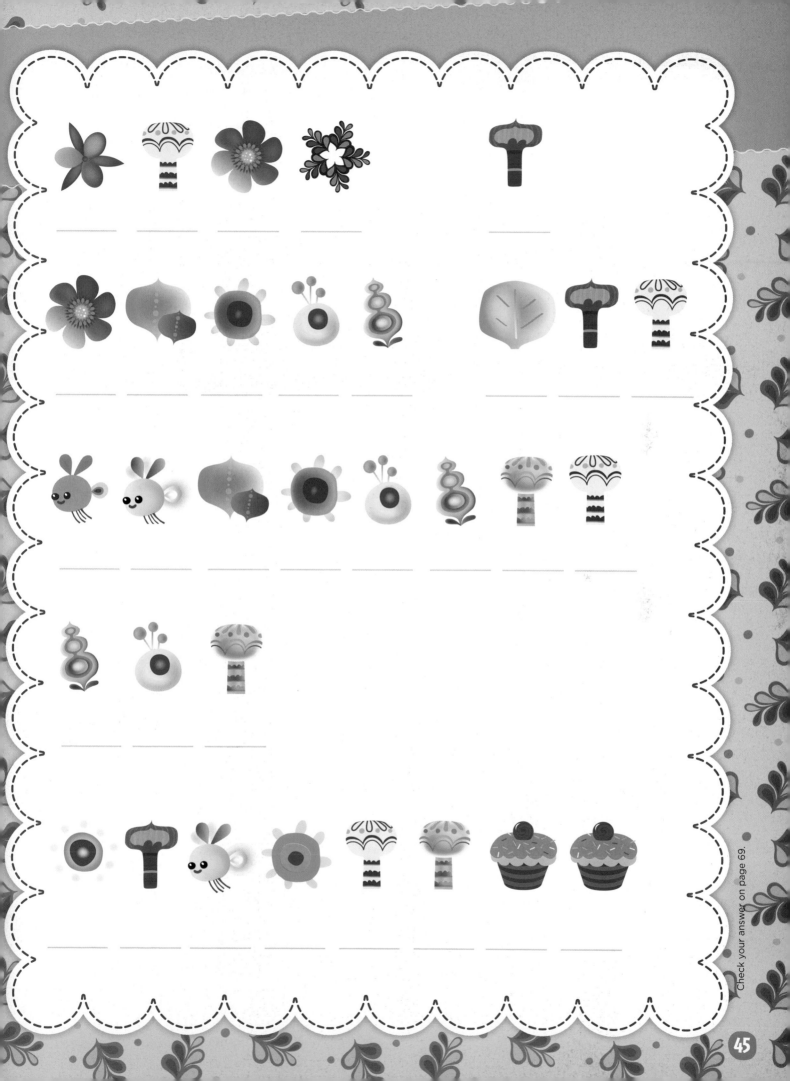

Check your answer on page 69.

Troll Tree TANGLE

Can you help King Peppy lead his people out of the Troll Tree to freedom?

START

5+4

Do the sums and follow the correct answers to help find the way out to the forest.

9 11-6

7 2+8

7 2+6

5 14+6

6 7-3

3 6-4

20 7+5

19 8+5

4 2+2

7
a

13
b

12
c

14
d

9
e

Check your answer on page 69.

Wheel Words

DJ Suki's got in a bit of a spin and left a muddled-up message for Poppy.

START here!

FINISH here!

Follow the circle in a clockwise direction and write down every third letter in the spaces to read the message.

W_'_ ___ ___ _____

__ __ ____ ____ ____

____ ___!

Check your answer on page 69.

Get to know ME!

What kind of Troll would you like to be? Get doodling and scribbling and let everyone know all about your true Troll self!

The TROLL I'm like is:

Take the test on pages 50–51

My Troll name is:

My True Colours are:

Scribble your favourite colours here

Things I like:

My Troll BFFS are called:

Things I'm really good at:

My hair-mazing
Troll hairstyle

Things I don't like:

_____

_____

_____

My favourite song is:

_____

49

Find Your TRUE TROLL

Take this test to find out which kind of Troll you're most like.

START

Do you like to let everyone know how you're FEELING?

NO → Do your friends often come to you for ADVICE?

YES →

NO → Do you like to SING?

Do your friends often come to you for ADVICE?

YES → Do you often get DISTRACTED EASILY?

NO →

Do you like to SING?

NO

YES →

Do you often get DISTRACTED EASILY?

YES ↓

NO →

Are you the first one of your friends to SHARE THEIR IDEAS?

NO

YES

You're like **CYBIL!**

Calm and always ready with words of wisdom for a friend!

50

Are you very CREATIVE?

NO

YES

Do you love a GOOD HUG?

NO

Do you like BEING OUTDOORS?

NO

You're like
HARPER!
Creative and exciting. An artist through and through.

YES

You're like
KARMA!
Down to earth and practical. You really care for the world around you.

YES

Is there anything better than a GOOD DANCE?

YES

Are you a real ANIMAL LOVER?

YES

NO

NO

You're like
POPPY!
OMG, you're full of energy, fun and hugs! What a Troll!

HOME Is Where the HAIR Is

Each Troll has very different hair and uses it to help show their True Colours. Can you figure out whose hair is whose?

Write the name of each Troll under the hair which you think belongs to them.

- **Poppy**
- **Branch**
- **Cooper**
- **Smidge**
- **Harper**
- **Biggie**
- **Guy Diamond**
- **DJ Suki**

a

b

Chapter 3:
True Colours

Poppy and her friends just won't give up on Creek, so they quietly crawl into King Gristle's room looking for the pendant.

"There it is!" whispers Cooper, pointing. While the King is distracted, Branch bravely sneaks over to open the pendant and free Creek.

But the pendant is stuck on King Gristle's cloak! Struggling to free it, the Trolls don't realise that the King's fearsome pet, Barnabus, has spotted them until it's almost too late ...

"Uh-oh!" gulps Branch. "Run for it!"

Hopping into the roller skate Bridget left behind, the Trolls zoom out of the room, with Barnabus hot on their heels!

As they skid around a corner, Poppy drops the pendant, and it flies into Barnabus' mouth!

"Creek!" screams Poppy in despair. Luckily, Barnabus smashes into a wall, spitting out the pendant. Poppy and her friends quickly open it and find that it's empty ... just as Chef catches them and locks them in a cage!

Things are looking bad, but they get even worse when Chef reveals her cunning plan ...

Creek wasn't eaten – he actually made a deal with Chef and is going to lead her to Troll Town in return for his life!

"Creek, you can't!" cries Poppy, as he takes away her cowbell and heads off. But it's too late.

Out in the forest, Creek uses the familiar sound of Poppy's cowbell to make the Trolls think everything is safe. So they all come out of hiding ... and right into the waiting arms of Chef, who snatches them all up!

Back in Bergen Town, as Poppy and her friends lose faith, their colours all drain away. Just then Branch starts to sing and suddenly his Troll friends have new hope.

"Well, we danced and sang and hugged. Now what?" asks Poppy.

"Now you get out of here!" sniffs Bridget, wiping a tear from her eye.

When she heard Branch's song, Bridget felt so sorry for the Trolls. After the Trolls helped her have such a great time with the King, Bridget realises Bergens don't need to eat Trolls to be happy, and helps the Trolls escape even though it puts her in danger.

Meanwhile, King Gristle refuses to start the Trollstice feast until Lady Glittersparkles arrives. As Chef tries to get him to change his mind, she finds that the Trolls have gone!

"What happened?" she yells.

"I let them go!" replies Bridget bravely.

Furious, Chef is about to have Bridget locked up when the Trolls suddenly return. Scampering onto Bridget they arrange themselves as a wig – once more turning her into Lady Glittersparkles!

King Gristle realises just how happy he

was with her. Maybe Bergens *don't* need to eat Trolls to be happy!

Chef can't believe it and tries to take over, but the Bergens arrest her instead!

Poppy and her friends had changed the Bergens' minds through the power of song and dance. Now the Bergens would never again need to eat another Troll to be happy!

"Everything you need to be happy is all around you," smiles Poppy, "and it always has been."

The End!

Show Your TROLL POWER

Think you're a Trolls expert? Then take this quiz and see how much you know about these hairy heroes and their world.

1. Where do the Trolls live?

- **a** Trolltopolis
- **b** Trollville
- **c** Troll Town

2. Which Troll is this?

- **a** Poppy
- **b** Branch
- **c** Harper

3. What is the name of Biggie's pet caterpillar?

- **a** Mr Dinkles
- **b** Mr Sprinkles
- **c** Geoff

4. What colour are the flowers on Poppy's headband?

- **a** Pink
- **b** Yellow
- **c** Blue

5. True or False?

King Gristle loves roller skating.

6. True or False?

Branch loves hugs.

7. Whose hair is this?

a Cooper

b Smidge

c Guy Diamond

8. Which part of Smidge is super strong?

a Her teeth

b Her feet

c Her hair

9. What colour is Chenille?

a Pink

b Blue

c Yellow

10. What are the Trolls' neighbours called?

a Dergens

b Fergens

c Bergens

Check your answers on page 69.

BONUS: FOR TOUGH TROLLS ONLY!

What is the name of the HOLIDAY when Chef makes Troll meatloaf?

Score 2 points if you're correct

How did you SCORE?

More than 9:
Get your hair on and join Poppy and her friends. You're a real Troll's Troll.

Between 4 and 9:
There's a Troll inside you just waiting to get out!

Less than 4:
Not bad, but you've still got a way to go to let your True Colours show.

HUG TIME!

Bring on the hugs! Look closely at the page and try to remember where all the Trolls are. Now close your eyes and tap the page with a pen 10 times. How many Trolls can you hit with a hug?

No hugs here! Lose 2 points if you hugged Branch.

SHOW YOUR TRUE COLOURS

dance

hug

sing

DreamWorks Trolls

Scrapbook Sudoku

Branch can't finish Poppy's puzzle. Can you help by drawing the correct pictures in the gaps, making sure there is only one of each picture in each row and column?

Check your answer on page 69.

make a
BEST FRIEND CARD

Spread the happy and create a super card for your best friend!

You'll need:

- Safe scissors
- Glue
- Stiff card, like an old cereal box
- Coloured pens or pencils
- String or wool
- Coloured paper
- Some old newspaper
- Glitter
- A grown-up to help

1 Carefully cut out the page opposite and stick it to the stiff card.

2 Spread out some old newspaper and get ready to create!

3 Colour the pictures with your brightest colours.

4 To make curly hair for your Trolls, tightly wind some strips of coloured paper around a pencil. Or you can stick on some string or wool to make fluffy hair.

5 Stick some patches of glue on your card and sprinkle it with glitter. Then carefully tip off the loose glitter and leave to dry.

6 When it's dry, fold your card along the pink line, write a message inside and give it to your friend!

Make sure you've finished reading your book BEFORE you CUT anything out!

Have a Happy Hair Day!

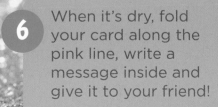

Have a Happy Hair Day!

Have a Happy Hair Day!

Have a
Happy Hair Day!

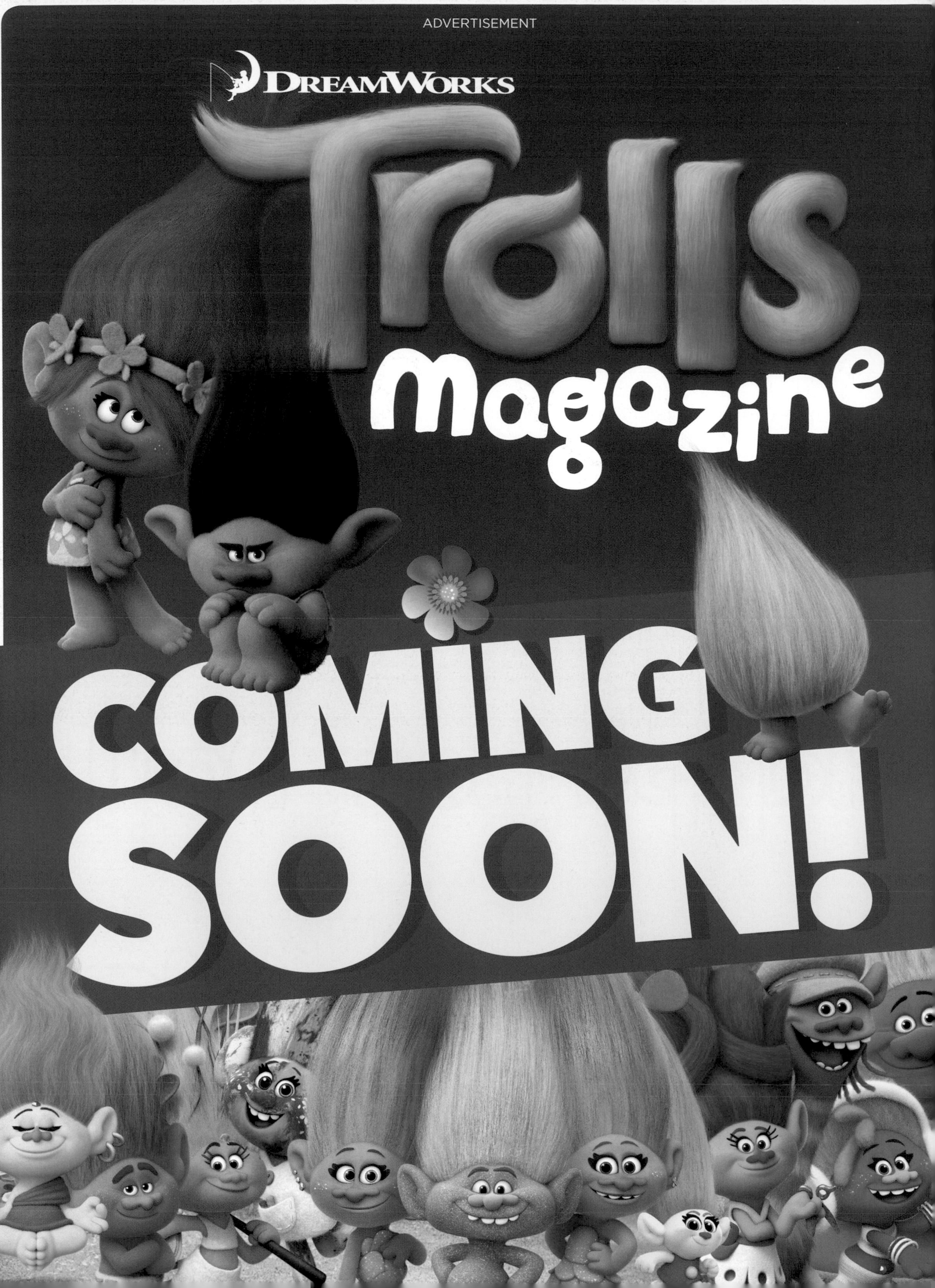
ADVERTISEMENT
DreamWorks
Trolls
Magazine
COMING SOON!

Join the dots to
finish the picture of

SUPER
SMIDGE

Answers

PAGES 8–9: Get to Know Poppy

Poppy gave out 22 hugs.
She hugged **Biggie** (**a**) the most.

PAGES 10–11: Get to Know Branch

Branch should take path **c**.

PAGE 17: The Show Must Go On

e	t	s	a	t	b	h	t	r	i	r	h	n	n	e
i	l	n	b	a	t	c	s	f	l	h	e	t	e	o
h	h	l	r	e	e	n	u	r	i	e	g	u	i	q
a	u	e	i	e	t	a	r	n	o	s	o	r	g	f
r	o	s	o	n	a	r	s	a	e	d	a	i	g	e
p	e	r	t	m	e	b	r	e	p	o	o	c	i	e
e	h	s	t	e	t	h	o	t	s	e	h	g	b	e
r	n	a	o	n	r	i	c	e	n	t	y	e	i	s
h	k	u	l	e	e	y	r	r	l	l	o	k	a	t
e	o	s	w	s	e	d	u	r	i	b	u	t	n	m
d	n	o	m	a	i	d	y	u	g	s	i	t	e	c
s	t	e	l	i	o	o	r	f	j	n	e	r	a	b
e	t	e	l	r	d	r	d	d	y	e	n	e	t	t
h	h	h	n	v	i	g	r	t	o	d	h	c	z	m
h	t	o	a	s	a	t	e	n	a	n	r	e	n	e

PAGE 18: Double Trouble

Harper has changed picture **d**.

PAGE 19: Who Needs a Hug?

Pieces **3, 4 & 7** don't appear in the picture.

PAGE 21: Nightmare Neighbour

PAGES 30–31 : Troll Teasers

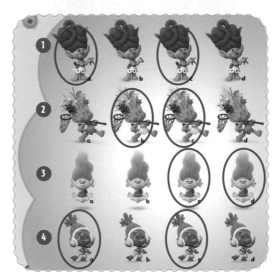

PAGE 32: Dancing in the Dark

Shadow **3**.

PAGES 34–35: Hide and Seek

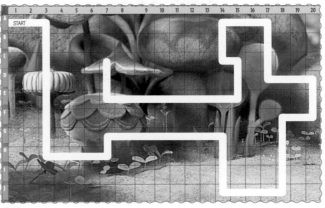

C7.

PAGES 36–37: Tasty Trolls

Path **c** leads to the Trolls.

PAGES 42–43: Search & Rescue

PAGES 44–45: Words of Wisdom

The message is: **Only a light can brighten the darkness.**

PAGE 46: Troll Tree Tangle

The correct path leads to **c**.

PAGE 47: Wheel Words

The message is:
We're all ready to Rock and Troll!

PAGES 52–53: Home Is Where the Hair Is

**a) DJ Suki; b) Poppy; c) Smidge;
d) Harper; e) Branch; f) Guy Diamond;
g) Cooper; h) Biggie.**

PAGES 56–57: Show Your Troll Power

**1: c) Troll Town; 2: b) Branch;
3: a) Mr Dinkles; 4: c) blue; 5: True;
6: False; 7: c) Guy Diamond; 8: c) Her hair;
9: b) blue; 10: c) Bergens; BONUS: Trollstice.**

PAGE 63: Scrapbook Sudoku